HEAVEN
SHINING THROUGH

HEAVEN
SHINING THROUGH

BY
JOE SICCARDI

To the Patrons of Seneca Falls
Library
May you always have
Heaven Shinin Through
Joe Siccardi

XULON PRESS

Xulon Press
2301 Lucien Way #415
Maitland, FL 32751
407.339.4217
www.xulonpress.com

Printed in the United States of America.

Edited by Xulon Press

ISBN-13: 9781545624562

DEDICATION

I FIRST SAW her jumping rope with her sister on a side street in Paterson, NJ. I wasn't impressed with the twiggy teen. We did, however, become friends and with each encounter I became more enamored with her – a juxtaposition of innocence and street smarts. Soon we became close friends where I marveled at her wit and wisdom and I was honored and blessed when she agreed to be my wife.

Through 40 years of marriage I was a witness to this amazing, complex woman ... sometimes child-like and other times speaking with the wisdom that comes with maturity. She was content yet vulnerable yet strong ... compassionate and passionate ... anxious yet content ... realistically optimistic ... unconditionally loving and caring ... sentimental yet grounded ... cheerful and sad ... content yet restless ... insecure yet secure ... self-effacing yet confident.

She was always supportive of me in all I did and followed me around the country as I sought the next best job along my career path. She was quick to reprimand with love when I strayed too far and showered me with love and support as we tackled new adventures. I loved her just for being her ... the way she was. And I know she loved me for just being me ... the way I was.

Our faults are what made us strong. In our imperfections, we were perfect ... because we did it all together.

There is no one else I would rather dedicate this book to.

My wife, my lover, my forever friend – for all our yesterdays, todays and throughout eternity

Karen Maureen (Corey) Siccardi

CHAPTER ONE

I DROVE ALONE on the black asphalt, which looked darker because of ominous clouds on the horizon ranging from dark gray to puffs of white. Out of the corner of my eye, I caught a glimpse of white as the sun tried to peek out from behind the clouds. It didn't succeed at first, but a ray rained into the picture, followed by a halo of rays.

My name is Samantha, but this is not the beginning of my story.

As I caught the rays, my mind drifted back to a time I drove my preschoolers to swimming practice. There was a similar canvas in the sky that day. They thought the light was heaven shining through. It was interesting they made that connection, considering we were not a church family at the time. It did, however, lead to a brief discussion about Jesus and heaven.

I didn't know why that thought had entered my mind at this moment. My children are well past preschool age. I miss those simple times when we had special moments to be present with each other. The time spent driving children to and from their events had been priceless. As they grew, the busyness of life seemed to intrude into our lives.

The rays disappeared as quickly as they had appeared as the clouds stitched themselves closer together, and I was once again left with just the asphalt and the clouds. The darkness sucked away the happy memories. I was driving toward the darkest patch of clouds, and I was in no hurry to return to my girlhood home. There weren't always happy memories, and I knew I would have to face those demons again.

As I turned off the interstate, I could feel my body tense. The landscape was eerily familiar yet distinctly different. There was the corner deli, the bakery, and the bars. Some had different names now, but they were the same bars nonetheless. The bank complex took up a square block. The cookie-cutter homes looked the same.

I pulled into the driveway, the same one I had pulled out of so many years ago. I grabbed my old key and opened the front door.

"Hi, Mom," I said, spotting Mom on the couch. She looked up and nodded, then quickly looked back at her crossword puzzle. I wasn't quite sure whether it was her grief or her disinterest in my return that had spurred her apathy.

I looked in the kitchen and saw a pile of dishes on the counter by the sink. "Maybe I'll just do some dishes."

"Whatever. Let me finish my puzzle in peace," Mom fired back.

I went to the kitchen, ran some water, and placed some of the dishes in the soapy water, drifting back to the past.

CHAPTER TWO

I THOUGHT I had a normal childhood. Dad was the light of my life, my biggest fan and supporter, and I was his little girl.

Mom and I had a different relationship. Even when I was a young girl, there was tension between us. I always sought her approval, but Mom was critical. I could get almost all A's and B's and Mom would focus on my lone C. I could get all dressed up and she would tell me my dress was wrinkled. She didn't like my friends or my music, and she always dismissed my opinions. To top it off, no matter what happened, the whole town knew about it. Mom liked to "share" at the beauty parlor, the grocery store, at church – everywhere! Unfortunately, her version of events didn't always mirror reality.

Still, Mom was a great cook. She could make anything taste good. She wasn't an accomplished chef, but she had learned her kitchen skills from her mom, who had learned from her mom. Recipes were guidelines, and Mom always knew when to add a pinch of this or cut back on that. She included me in the kitchen, firmly teaching me the basics early on and sharing her skills as I grew up.

I always followed Mom around the kitchen, and I soon learned about her critical nature. However, one time when I was about five years old, she handed me an apron and had me help mix the chocolate chips into the cookie dough. This was a monumental task for a five-year-old, and a good deal of the batter ended up on my once-clean apron. I started to cry, but Mom scooped me up in her arms and said, "Sam, that's okay. That's why we wear aprons when we cook." When it came to the kitchen and cooking skills, Mom was open and forgiving.

I sailed through elementary school and high school. In fact, I graduated in the top five of my class at Our Lady Queen of Peace High School. I always thought this was quite an accomplishment, but Mom always added, "Of course, there were only sixty-six graduates."

I was well liked in high school, but I never did a lot of dating. It's hard to "find" someone at an all-girl school. The few times I did go out, Mom always embarrassed me in front of my date, and I never went out with the same boy twice.

My best friends from grade school, Mary Bernadette (whom we called "Bernie"), Betty, Lynn, and Pat, loved to come over, especially when Mom went on a cooking spree. Bernie, Betty, and Lynn went to Our Lady Queen of Peace, but Pat was the "rebel" who went to public school. Mom always picked on her too.

I learned my way around the kitchen during those preteen and teen years, and Mom was always there to coach me through a lunch or dinner, although my dishes never quite measured up to her standards.

Because of my grades, I could go just about anywhere, being accepted at a number of major colleges. I chose the College of Mount Saint Vincent's nursing program although the sight of blood made me sick. It was a case of trying to please everyone but myself.

Over Mom's objections, Dad bought me a red Mustang convertible for graduation for my daily commute to The Bronx. It was my independence. Once I had those keys in my hands, I was never home. It was off with my girls, often ending up at the hot dog joint to flirt with the guys.

After graduation, the Fearsome Fivesome was heading off in different directions. Bernie was off to cosmetology school and the workplace. Lynn was going to school at Fairleigh Dickinson, while Betty was headed to the sunshine at the University of Miami. We already lost Pat from our pack when she moved to Rochester, NY.

But we were solid that summer. We all started working – I worked at the local bakery – but whenever we had the chance, it was off to the Jersey Shore in our bikinis and cutoff jeans. Coyly watching and teasing boys on the boardwalk at Seaside Heights was a staple of the summer.

Summer raced by too quickly, and it came time to say a tearful good-bye to Betty as she headed to the Sunshine State. Although Bernie and Lynn were staying around, I knew life was changing and would never be the same, but I was determined to savor every minute.

My freshman year in college was, well, less-than-stellar. Between the commute, the challenges of college, and my newfound freedom with my Mustang, I saw unrecognizable grades. So, as a vibrant eighteen-year-old, I did the natural thing: party! Of course, my lifestyle choice did not sit well with Mom, but I was comfortable "getting by" in class and enjoying life on weekends.

It all came to a head one February Saturday night. I returned home from a date around midnight only to be greeted by Mom. She informed me I had not one but two calls from different boys while I was "out doing God-knows-what with a third."

I was proud of my popularity until she blurted out, "What are my friends going to think? I'm raising the town whore!"

That stung, although I'm still not sure whether it was because she had categorized herself as a victim or used the hurtful slur. Our verbal sparring – and volume – escalated from there, with both of us hurling insults and saying way more than we should have. Dad even had to come in and send us to separate corners while he tried to sort out the mess. Poor Dad. He had to listen to Mom's blathering, and then he had to confront me. Both of us were crying.

"Dad, she had no right to say that," I sobbed. "I've never done anything wrong."

And I never did. Sure, I liked to party and toy with guys. I was, admittedly, a flirt, and I enjoyed leading guys on, but my upbringing and my four years with the nuns at Our Lady Queen of Peace made me a controlled woman who knew when to put the brakes on in a relationship. A few guys never came back because of this, but that was okay. If a guy wasn't interested in more than my body and wasn't willing to give me his heart, soul, and undivided attention, then good riddance.

A couple of months later, I sat with Bernie for days on end when she thought she was pregnant. Her "boyfriend" had skipped out as soon as the subject of fatherhood was broached, so it was up to me to hold her hand, hug her, comfort her, and wipe her tears.

"What did I do?" "What am I going to do?" she said. "Why did I listen to him when he told me he loved me?"

It turned out to be a false alarm, but the experience steeled my will to stay in control of my life.

And then came Chad.

CHAPTER THREE

I FIRST MET Chad at – where else? – a club. Bernie, Betty, Lynn, and I had decided to have a girl's night out to celebrate. We were celebrating Betty's return from Miami and the nineteenth birthdays of Lynn (May 16) and me (June 20). We headed to Greenwood Lake since New York's drinking age was eighteen back in the mid-60s. We were determined to let our hair down and have some fun.

I spotted Chad as I walked in the door, although I had never seen him before. He was at a corner table, and our eyes met for a brief moment. I quickly turned away to giggle with the girls about the "eye candy".

We settled in at a table near the dance floor and ordered a round. We were surveying the club, bobbing to the Four Seasons' "Workin' My Way Back To You," when a guy came over and asked me to dance. I never said no to a dance, so off we went to the dance floor. What happened next, though, caught me off guard.

"You dance well," he said. "I'm Jimmy."

"Thank you. My name is Sam."

"Do you girls come here often?"

"Not really. This is a special occasion. We haven't seen Betty in almost a year, and Pat's birthday was last week. It's legal to drink at eighteen in New York, so here we are."

"I'm not going to keep you from your girls, but did you notice that guy over there at the table?" Jimmy asked.

I looked over and said, "Yeah."

"He would really like to meet you."

"So, why didn't he come over and ask me to dance?"

"Because he's a dunderhead."

I stopped in my tracks.

"I'll introduce you if you want. He's a nice guy; he's just a little on the shy side. He said you were cute."

I thought about it for a second or so, then waved my hand in disbelief as I walked back to the table, saying, "I ... I don't know. This is pretty bizarre. Are you serious?"

"Yeah. Yeah. If you introduce me to the girls at your table, I'll introduce you to Chad."

Bernie greeted me with, "What's wrong, sunshine? Is he bothering you?"

"He wants me to meet his friend," I explained.

Jimmy interjected with, "Chad, the one with the short, dusty hair and five-o'clock shadow over there in the corner."

"And you're having reservations?" questioned Bernie.

"Are you nuts? He's gorgeous! I'll meet him," echoed Betty.

"Don't let us stop you," added Lynn.

Jimmy piped in, "I would be more than happy to keep you girls company."

"Works for me!" said Bernie.

"Me too," added Betty.

"We're here to have some fun. Go ahead. Have some fun!" Lynn encouraged.

"I just ... I ... I don't know. This is pretty strange."

The girls give me that "go ahead" look. Jimmy raises his hand as if to say, "Well?"

I gave in. "Okay, I guess. I'll give him ten minutes."

"Great. Yeah. If you introduce me to the girls, I'll introduce you to Chad," said a triumphant Jimmy.

We got to Chad's table, and he stood up. Man, he was even better-looking up close with sandy blonde hair, brown eyes with flecks of green, a rugged face with a hint of a five-o'clock shadow, and the physique of a Greek god. He looked somewhat surprised to see me with Jimmy. He shook my hand and said, "Hi. I'm Chad, and you're the most beautiful girl I've seen in here tonight."

All I could blurt out was, "Sam. Samantha. Samantha Casey, but they call me Sam."

"It's a pleasure meeting you, Samantha," he said extending his hand. "Sam."

Holding my hand tighter, he responded, "Chadwick Watt. They call me Chad."

The barmaid arrived and asked if we wanted anything. "I'll have what he's having," I said, and Chad told her another Coke, adding, "I'm the designated driver."

"So am I," I laughed, although the Coke I had brought from my table may have had a little Bacardi in it.

We sat there for the next four hours, just talking. He'd just completed his junior year, studying engineering at nearby Manhattan College. He was also from northern New Jersey, although he had an apartment with three other Manhattan students in The Bronx, including Jimmy. He was open, and he appeared to be honest. He didn't talk much about himself, instead wanting to know about me. And he listened. I know because he would occasionally bring up something I had mentioned earlier in our conversation. And he seemed to love moving my hair from my eyes after a laugh. It was the first time in my life I'd felt so at ease with a guy.

As the evening waned, I asked Chad if he wanted to dance. "I'm not much of a dancer," he replied, but when "When a Man Loves a Woman" started playing, I got up, took Chad's hand, and led him to the dance floor, where Bernie and Jimmy were dancing.

"Come on," I said. "They can't be the only ones dancing."

"I'm warning you. Your toes are in danger."

"I'm not worried. So what if you step on a few toes? I have ten. Besides, this is nice and slow." I put my head on Chad's shoulder and whispered, "You're doing great."

"You make it easy."

As the song ended, I gave Chad a peck on the cheek. "Thank you."

"No. Thank you!"

"Does that make this our song?" I asked.

"I hope so."

A little after midnight, the girls started getting rowdy, so I told Chad I should probably get them home. "Okay," he said. "I'll walk you out to your car."

He held my hand as we walked to the parking lot. I gave the girls the keys so they could get settled in. We got to the car, and he said, "This was fun. I'm so glad I got a chance to meet you."

He surprised me again. I was expecting a kiss, but instead he brushed back my hair and gave me a peck on the cheek. Then he whispered in my ear, "Can I call you sometime?"

"Sure," was all I could muster. I reached into the car of giggling girls to give him my number. Bernie had already written it down, and she handed it to me. I gave it to Chad, and he kissed me.

I didn't have to wait long. The next morning around eleven, the phone rang. Mom answered and handed me the phone.

"Who is it?" I asked.

"I don't know! Another guy. What else is new?"

"Mom!" After a brief pause, I said, "Hello," to a voice laughing. "Chad?

"Yeah, it's me."

"I'm so sorry about that. I told you my mom doesn't have a filter."

"That's fine. Really. I just wanted to call and tell you I really enjoyed talking with you last night."

"It was fun. You were easy to talk to."

13

"What are you doing?" he asked.

"Bernie and I were just getting ready to go to the mall. Do you have any plans for the day?"

"Not for the day, but I was wondering what you were doing tonight."

"Tonight?"

Bernie walked into the kitchen and realized who I was talking to. For the rest of the conversation, she teased me – you know, mouthing "Chad" and going into a pantomime faint, or mouthing "I love you" and hugging herself in a mock embrace. So there I was, trying to hush her and listen to him.

Finally he said he wouldn't keep me, but asked if he could see me. "I'll plan something, if that's okay," he said. "I'd love to see you again. Pick you up about six? We'll grab a bite to eat."

"Well, sure," I responded, twirling my hair – something I had never done before. "Where are we going?"

"I have something in mind," he said. "See you around six."

"Wait ... what should I wear? Casual? Dressy?" I stammered as Bernie continued to mock me.

"You would look great in rags," he said. "Just dress comfortably. Nothing special."

As I hung up, Bernie grabbed me like a schoolgirl. "Aw, you like him, don't you?" she said. She danced around the kitchen, singing, "Sammy's got a boyfriend. Sammy's got a boyfriend."

"Stop. I do not," I protested, although I could feel my face flushing the shade of my highlights. "I have nothing to wear! Let's go. I'll pick up some new jeans and a top at the mall."

Of course, Bernie had to let Betty and Lynn know before we left, and the four of us met at the mall to do some power shopping. The three of them teased me all afternoon, but they helped me pick out some jeans and a cute top, new nail polish, and lipstick. They all came back to the house to help me get ready. As the polish dried and the last hair was put in place, they said, "Awww," in unison.

At six almost on the dot, the doorbell rang. Betty ran out of the room, but she couldn't get to the door before Mom.

"Good evening, Mrs. Casey. I'm Chad," he said, extending his hand.

Mom smiled and said, "You must be here for Sam. Come in."

"She's just about ready," chimed Betty, giving me the cue to make my grand entrance.

Before Mom could start her inquisition, I walked out. "Wow, you look beautiful," he said, then he turned to Mom and said, "I see where Sam gets her beauty."

I saw Mom blush. I had never seen that before.

"We won't be too late," he added as I gently pushed him out the door.

"See you later, Mom," I said, leaving poor Betty to field what I knew was going to be a million questions.

Chad continued to be a perfect gentleman. We walked arm in arm to the car, and he even opened the door. He drove us to my favorite hot dog joint. *How did he know I loved Falls View?* I thought. *Oh, yeah, I mentioned it last night. Wow, he was listening!* He ordered me two dogs all the way, Frenchies well done, and birch beer, looked at me with a wink, and said, "Right?" *Wow, he really did listen.*

From there we headed to Bowl-O-Mat for a night of bowling. Now, I had never bowled in my life, so it was an experience. Chad told me it was easy: you just roll the ball down the alley and knock down the pins. It felt good when he wrapped his arms around me to show me how to hold the ball. I think my high score was around a twenty-six, but we had fun laughing, playing, and talking.

The night was still young, and I wondered what was next as we walked back to the car hand in hand. The surprises continued. We drove up to Garret Mountain and parked in an area overlooking the city affectionately known as Lover's Cove; it was a place I had been to before a number of times. *This is it,* I thought. *Let the real Chad show up.*

He went to the trunk, pulled out a blanket, and carefully placed it on the hood. Then he opened my door, took my hand, led me to the blanket, and helped me up. There we sat under the twinkling stars overlooking the twinkling city lights, holding hands and talking, oblivious to the steamy windows of the cars around us. I didn't want it to end.

The night ended, but our relationship didn't. Instead, it continued to grow throughout that summer. Chad and I spent a lot of time together and got to know each other better, and he never wore off. He saw me at my worst when I had a summer cold, but he still said I was beautiful. He put up with my moods, gently turning my sour side into a sweeter one with just the right phrase or joke. He encouraged and challenged me every time we went out.

By summer's end, I was smitten with him, and it appeared to be mutual. After all, for most of the summer, where he was, I was. We went to the shore and the movies, went on long drives, and parked on Garret Mountain. We learned a lot about each other but still knew our boundaries. Sure, there was plenty of holding hands, hugging, kissing, and even a little fondling, but we both knew when to slow down. I think that's what I loved about him – yes, I said "loved." He listened patiently to my words and my heart. He gave me his prime time, not the leftovers. He praised me. He surprised me. He courted me. He treated me like a queen in front of other people.

I learned that Chad was focused on his career, both in engineering and the Air Force. He talked about how he could blend both after graduation. He took his studies seriously, so I wasn't sure where our relationship would go when school started again.

It changed, but not all that much. Even though we went to school near each other in The Bronx, we lived in different states, so phone calls were expensive. Yet he found a way to keep in touch. He would call just to say, "I love you!" "I was thinking about you!" or "I miss you!" He always planned either a Friday- or Saturday-night date, usually in the city. He scheduled study dates either at the library or his place – and forced me to study! We went to ball games, museums, and plays in the city or took long walks in Riverside Park or Van Cortlandt Park.

My mom invited him and his family to Thanksgiving dinner, and they accepted. It went well, although she managed to embarrass me over and over with her questions and her revelations about my childhood. ("She was a cute baby; do you want to see some pictures?" "She was shy and awkward." "She was book smart, but she didn't have much common sense.")

Thankfully, Chad rescued me, "reminding" me we had promised to meet up with Bernie and Jimmy. In the middle of traffic, he pulled the car over, took my hand, and said, "You know I love you. Every day I love you more. But I have to know if you feel the same way."

"Yes! Yes! Without a doubt!" I screamed, grabbing his head in my hand and planting a long, deep kiss on his lips.

From that moment on, it was official. We were a couple. It appeared that Bernie and Jimmy were also a couple, although we were too engrossed in ourselves to even notice.

Not much changed as went through the rest of the school year. We still had to get through his stint with the Air Force, and I still had two more years of school, so we never talked about the future or marriage. In fact, we never talked about getting engaged either. Still, he would indulge my fantasies when we walked past a jewelry store or bridal shop, always with a big grin on his face.

I stayed at his apartment a couple of times during the winter when the weather got bad, sleeping in his bed alone. He wouldn't have it any other way. By February, I started keeping some clothes at his place so I could get ready "properly" if we went into the city. During spring break,

18

I went with Chad and his family to Florida, and I was so proud to be his escort to a military ball just before his graduation. Tears of joy were in my eyes as he walked up to receive his degree.

We only had a few weeks between graduation and his assignment at Wright-Patterson Air Force Base in Ohio. Two weekends before he had to leave, I decided to cook him dinner while Mom and Dad were out of town for the weekend visiting relatives in Delaware, even though I had never prepared an entire meal by myself. I made chicken chasseur (baked chicken breast in a tarragon mushroom sauce) with glazed carrots, pommes anna, and French bread. I had a bottle of Bordeaux I had picked up on my way back from school a few weeks earlier. I also made a pumpkin and pecan cheesecake.

Chad was right on time, as usual. The table was set, but I was still in my sauce-stained apron with hints of flour dusting my hair. I lit the candles, told Chad to get comfortable, freshened up, and served dinner. It was magical. The chicken was moist and tasty, and the French bread the perfect accompaniment for the sauce. The Bordeaux was the perfect pairing.

After dessert, we went to the couch to talk and cuddle. I don't know if it was the intoxicating effect of the wine or the realization that this all was ending, but I wanted to go further than just kissing. As I started unbuttoning his shirt, he asked, "Are you sure about this?" to which I responded, "Definitely." I led his hand to the buttons on my blouse. This was new territory for both of us: skin on skin.

I got up to take off my jeans, then reached out to him and led him to my bedroom.

"Are you sure about this?" he asked again.

"Definitely," I responded. And there in my bed, we made love, both exploding in ecstasy. We lay in each other's arms for what felt like hours. Eventually he rolled over and dozed off. I just kept staring at him, my head resting on my hand.

But as the euphoria waned and the afterglow ebbed, second thoughts crept into my mind. I felt what we had done was right, but my upbringing nagged my thoughts. *What did I do? What am I going to do? Why did I listen to him when he told me he loved me? He's leaving next week. Is he going to leave me now? What did I do?*

There I was, literally and figuratively stuck buck-naked between a wall and a man. How had an in-control woman lost so much control?

As I lay staring, Chad woke up. He rolled over, kissed my arm, then propped his head on his hand and kissed me. "You okay?" he asked.

"Yes," I responded. "I just have to pee." I bolted up and grabbed a blanket to hide my nakedness on my way to the bathroom. I threw in a towel for Chad from the bathroom.

When I was returned, Chad was already getting dressed. *I knew it,* I thought to myself. He asked me again if I was all right, then said he should probably be going.

"I don't want to give the neighbors anything to talk about," he said as we walked toward the door. As he kissed me good-night, he said, "You do know I love you."

As his taillights faded down the street, I convinced myself my actions had ruined a perfect relationship. I put on some floppy sweats, made myself a cup of tea, and wrapped myself in a blanket on the couch. The minute hand on the clock inched ever so slowly. Twelve after ... what felt like forever ... thirteen after ... another eternity ... fourteen after ... With each minute, another argument raged in my mind. *What we did was right. What we did was wrong. What did I do? What am I going to do? When will daylight come so I can call Bernie?* I needed her, and I needed her *now*.

Shortly after eight o'clock, I made the call. Bernie's mom answered and got her for me. She was still half asleep when she answered, but as soon as I said, "Bern," she knew something was wrong and immediately became alert.

"What's wrong, Sam? What's wrong?"

As I started to blurt out, "I think I messed –" she cut me off. "I'll be there in a half hour."

She walked through the door and found me crying, curled up on the couch. I reached up to her and burst into a fresh round of tears. She sat down next to me and hugged me. "Calm down, Sam. Tell me what happened."

Through a box of tissues, I told her everything that had happened, from dinner to our love-making. She never said a word; she just kept the tissues coming. After I finished my tale, she said, "Did it feel right?"

"Yes," I sobbed. "No." Then I shrugged my shoulders and said, "I don't know."

"Well, do you love him?" she asked.

"Yes, but that's the problem. I don't know if he still loves me."

"What makes you say that?" she asked. "Did he say something?"

"No," I whimpered. "He said he loved me, but he went home."

"Okay," Bernie said. "You're thinking too hard. You guys have been going out for a year –"

I interrupted her. "I know, but we never went all the way. He knew I wanted to wait, and I thought he wanted to wait. But we got caught up in the moment, and one thing led to another, and now I'm afraid he's gone."

"That's silly," she said. "I've seen you two together. He not only loves you, but he respects you too. That's more than a lot of guys –"

"But," I interrupted again, "that's the problem. I don't know if he will still respect me."

"Well, maybe you should talk to him," Bernie offered. "Come on, enough of this pity party. We can't change the past. You know that. Hell, you told me that, remember? But you can still control the future. You're the same fun-loving girl you were yesterday," she said, then put on an infectious smile and added, "only today, you're a woman," as she poked my arm.

She was right, of course, but I was positive Chad would soon be history. He was leaving for Ohio the following week, and I would quickly become a memory.

22

When Chad called later in the day, the first thing he said was, "Are you okay? I sensed something was wrong when I left last night. I didn't mean to hurt you. Do you want to talk?"

"No, everything is fine. Last night was ... well ... special," I gushed. "I'm okay, just a little tired. How about a rain check?"

He tried to convince me to go out, but I continued to say no until he finally said, "Okay, Sam, but remember, I love you!"

That was Sunday. He tried again Monday and Tuesday. Each time, I found an excuse. I knew we should talk about that night, but I wasn't ready to. And with each passing day, I started insulating my heart from breaking.

On Wednesday night, Chad showed up at my door. He gave me a quick kiss, said hi to Mom and Dad, and tried to whisk me out the door. "Let's go for coffee," he said. At first I resisted, but Mom started asking questions, so off we went to the diner.

"Something is wrong," he said after the waitress brought our coffees. "Is this about Saturday?"

"No, nothing is wrong," I insisted.

"Bullshit!" he said, catching me off guard. I hadn't ever heard him say anything remotely off-color.

"No, no, everything is fine," I said. "Saturday ... was ... was ... wonderful. I guess you ... I guess I thought you should spend some time with your family since you're going to Ohio next week."

"I spend enough time with my family," he said. "I want to spend my time with you. But there is something else going on. I know you wanted to wait, and I'm sorry we didn't. I wanted to wait too. But it doesn't change anything. I love you even more."

"I know, and … it … was … great," I stuttered, grasping for each word. "I'm not sorry we made love. . ."

He interrupted me. "Yes, we made love. We did not just have sex." He put his hands on mine. "Sam, I love you."

"But you went home! You left me alone!"

Chad leaned back in his seat. "That's what this is about?"

Through tears, I blurted, "I … I guess so. I got scared that you didn't love me anymore."

Chad responded, "I … I didn't realize –"

"I didn't want to lose you, but I felt like you got what you wanted and I was … excess baggage."

"Excess baggage? You're the best thing that has ever happened to me. The truth is I was embarrassed. I knew you'd wanted to wait, and so had I. But we didn't, and I don't regret a minute."

"Me neither."

"Wow. I wish you would have told me this on Sunday. I was afraid too. I was afraid you had lost respect for me, and I didn't want to lose you. Sam, I love you!"

With that, he reached into his pocket and pulled out a little box. I opened it. In it were two white gold rings studded with small diamonds and soldered together with a big gap in the middle. I just looked at him with a quizzical expression on my face.

24

"That's the wedding ring I picked out for you," he said. He reached into his other pocket and pulled out another little box. I opened it. It was another white gold ring, this one with a diamond proudly standing in a simple yet elegant raised setting.

"That's the engagement ring I picked out for you," he added. He put the two settings together. "A perfect fit," he said. "Just like you and me. They were made for each other. Just like you and me."

I was speechless.

"Samantha Marie Casey, will you marry me?"

I was still speechless as the conversation at the table started to draw some attention.

"Samantha Marie Casey, will you marry me?" he repeated.

"Are you sure?"

"I'm positive. Samantha Marie Casey, will you marry me?"

"Yes! Yes!" I said through welled eyes. The crowd around us started clapping, and someone said, "Way to go," as I pushed my left hand out.

"No," Chad said.

The crowd stopped clapping. Someone whispered, "What did he say?" Our waitress dropped her coffee pot.

"Not sometime in the future," Chad continued. "I mean right now, this weekend. Sam, I love you. I don't want to wait to make you my wife."

As the clapping erupted again, I answered, "I love you too. This weekend it is!"

The claps turned into hugs and handshakes from total strangers. The couple in the booth next to ours picked up our check. Our waitress brought us a piece of cake she had cut into the shape of a heart. Even the cooks came into the dining area to offer their well wishes. There we were, two young lovers being treated like rock stars. Amid the commotion, we were isolated, existing just for each other.

For the rest of the evening, we planned our wedding. We agreed not to tell anyone, although Jimmy sort of knew what Chad was thinking. If Jim knew, Bernie knew. We both decided we wanted them to be a part our wedding. We agreed not to tell our parents or friends. We knew eloping would disappoint them, but this was our moment, and we didn't want any lectures. It was a little surreal. Both of us were more, well, practical.

Chad said he would make all the arrangements. He would pick me up early on Saturday morning and we would head to Maryland. All I needed to do was come up with a cover story; of course, spending the weekend with Bernie was perfect.

Even though it was late when I got home, I called Bernie. "Do you have some time tomorrow? We have to talk about something," I said.

She cut me off. "He did it, didn't he? He asked you to marry him! That son of a gun. I knew it. I knew it!"

"Well, yeah," I said. "That's why we have to talk. Tomorrow."

"I'll see you about nine," she said before she hung up.

I filled her in, and even romantic Bernie was impressed with the details. She said Jimmy had told her that Chad was going to ask me to marry him, but they thought it would be later that year. This weekend. Elope.

"I didn't see that coming with Chad," she said. "Okay, this is between us. We'll go shopping tomorrow. You'll be the most beautiful bride ever." She started to cry, and she hugged me. "You'll be the most beautiful bride ever."

On Friday we went to the mall. After looking at what seemed like hundreds of dresses, I picked a long white A-line satin dress with a crisscross chiffon bodice and a behind-the-neck tie. Bernie insisted I wear my hair up, and she found an orchid hairpiece that complemented the ensemble. Then we went into the lingerie department, where she picked out a short-style peignoir set as a gift to me. Both the gown and robe were embellished with embroidered lace and beads, and the gown had chiffon flounces on the sleeves and hem and a chiffon tie at the waist. The wrap robe also had a tie.

I spent Friday night at Bernie's house. Chad and Jimmy picked us up bright and early on Saturday, and as we entered the Garden State Parkway, I realized we were going through with this. We pulled into the parking lot at the Sutton Inn in Elkton, Maryland, around noon and checked in. Bernie and I went to one room and Jim and Chad went to the other so we could get ready.

By four, we were at the Historic Little Wedding Chapel. Chad looked dashing in his uniform, and he stared at me in my dress. As he took my hand, he whispered in my ear how incredibly beautiful I was and how incredibly proud he was that I was going to be his wife. With a simple "I do," I became Samantha Watt, Mrs. Chadwick Watt.

Following the ceremony, the four of us went to dinner. We were thankful for all Bernie and Jim had done for us, and we predicted they would be next. We left them around eight and retired to our room, which the inn staff had cleaned and freshened with rose petals on the king-size bed. They'd also left a bottle of champagne chilling.

We talked for awhile, figuring out how we were going to tell our parents, talking about where we would live, and fantasizing about our future together. Around ten, I went into the bathroom and walked out in my negligee. It did not stay on long, and this time it felt right – very right.

CHAPTER FOUR

THE FIRST THING Chad and I had to do was face our parents. We went to my house first. As we walked in the house, I called Mom from the kitchen and Dad from his upstairs workshop. When they gathered into the living room, I announced, "Mom, Daddy, Chad and I got married."

It felt like forever before either of them said anything, although it was just a matter of seconds. Mom broke the silence. "You did what? When? Where? What were you two thinking?" she asked in her usual animated manner. Before I could answer, she continued. "No! No! This is wrong! This is wrong! Are you pregnant?"

"No, Mom, I'm not pregnant, and this isn't wrong!" I responded.

"How could you do this to us?" she continued, oblivious to my words. She looked directly at Chad and said, "How could you do this? How could you take advantage of my daughter?"

"Mom," I interjected. "This was our decision. Not just Chad's. Ours."

"And what am I supposed to tell everybody? That my daughter got married and didn't care enough to tell me?"

"Mom, listen to yourself. Why do you always have to be the center of attention? Can't you be happy for us?"

"No," she said. "This is a mistake you'll regret for the rest of your life. After all we've done for you. You're so ungrateful."

Tears poured from my eyes as she turned away, waving her hands. Daddy stepped in. He was certainly shaken by the news, but he gave me a tearful hug and whispered, "I'll talk to Mom. I'll make her understand. We went through this exact same thing. We eloped just before I was deployed to Korea."

That was a story I had never heard before.

Then he gave me a bigger hug and said, "Congratulations! I love you. Don't ever forget that." He turned to Chad with an outstretched hand that evolved into a hug. "Welcome to the family, as crazy as it is. You just better make sure you take care of my little girl."

"I will, sir," Chad responded.

"Have you told your folks yet?" Dad asked, and when we told him they were next, he shooed us out the door. "Go. I'll take care of things here."

The ride to Chad's house was quiet. I was replaying the scene at my house over and over in my mind while Chad tried to calm me down.

"We've got each other, right?" he said. "I love you. No regrets."

Chad led the way into his house and called for his mom and dad. The scene was eerily similar, yet distinctively different. "Mom. Dad. I want to introduce you to my wife, Samantha Watt."

His mom started to cry, but without the histrionics. She reached out to me and grabbed my hand. "Let me see that ring," she said. "Welcome." Then she turned to Chad and gave him a playful punch in the arm. "You could have warned me," she said.

His dad was a little more reserved at first, but he quickly warmed up. "Congratulations, you two. I never would have thought you would just run off." He put his arm around his wife. As she looked up at him, he asked if my parents knew. When we related the story, he said, "I'll give Joe a call." His mom asked who else knew. So many questions. So few answers.

Both parents planned a dinner with us the next day. We agreed, but on our way back to the hotel, I told Chad we were being set up. "You know they want to separate us," I said.

"I know," said Chad, "but that's not going to happen."

Our dinner went just as expected. My mom, while cordial, said she felt I should stay at home while Chad "figured out the lay of the land" in Ohio. "Besides," she said, "you still have school. You're not going to throw away the past three years, are you?"

Dad, likewise, had a million reasons why his little girl should not go to Ohio. Chad's dad said he was willing to convert the garage and breezeway into an apartment for us, a project his mom fully endorsed. All four felt we should get married "in the eyes of God."

We listened, at first adamant about starting our lives together. But the constant "suggestions" started wearing us down – or, more accurately, Chad. After dessert, we gave them all hugs and kisses and headed back to the hotel.

That's when Chad said, "You know, they made some sense. I have to report for duty. I don't even know if I'll be allowed to go off the base right away. And I don't know anything about the Dayton area."

I, on the other hand, was quiet. I said little, and my eyes slowly welled with tears. Finally, I pulled my hand away and said to him, "Why did we even bother to get married?"

I guess you could say that was our first disagreement, just over two days after saying, "I do." I knew Chad was right, but I was hurt. I felt betrayed, especially since he had promised we wouldn't be separated.

We continued to discuss the issue at the hotel and reluctantly agreed I would stay home while he settled in Ohio. But I let him know in no uncertain terms I wasn't happy with the decision. We went to bed with a kiss and "I love you," but then simply went to sleep – or at least we pretended to sleep. On Tuesday, Chad headed to Ohio and I went back home.

I was adamant about moving to Dayton, and I immediately started making plans. I went to my guidance counselor at school, who worked with me to find another school in Ohio, Wright State University, where my credits and clinical time could be transferred.

I also learned a lot about being a military wife. While we were 99 percent certain that Chad would be assigned to Wright-Patterson, we hadn't expected him to leave for commissioned officer training at Maxwell Air Force Base in Alabama for a month. His mom, dad, brother, and I flew down for his graduation, and the two of us drove back to Dayton so we could do some apartment hunting. We found a nice little attic apartment just outside of the city just in time for me to rush home, pack up necessities, return, and get ready for my final year in college. It was a wild August.

Mom, of course, was livid. In fact, before I headed to Alabama, we had one of our traditional battles. How could I do this? Why was I shutting her out? What about having a church wedding? Didn't I care about anyone but myself?

When the reality of the move sunk in, Mom softened a little. Still, she stubbornly insisted we have a church wedding. Chad and I had talked about it; we were content with what we had done, but we agreed to a small gathering for family and friends over the Thanksgiving weekend. I relayed the information to Mom. I told her it was going to be small and simple, and that Chad and I were just going to show up. We would be too busy to plan a formal wedding.

She thought for a minute, then agreed. She and Chad's Mom would contact the church, plan the reception, and send out the invitations. All we had to worry about was the wedding party and showing up. Surprise – we ended up with a small, intimate wedding with over 250 guests! The moms had gotten carried away, although in retrospect it did turn out well. Of course, my Mom couldn't let my decision to wear my original wedding dress go without criticism.

Our first "home" was a three-room attic apartment, just big enough for the two of us. We learned so much there about each other, about ourselves, and about life in general. Chad learned a new language – "woman speak" – and expanded his vocabulary to include words like *period, PMS,* and *cramps.* He discovered Midol was a real product with a real purpose and uncovered the true meaning of mood swings. He didn't understand them, but he quickly recognized their existence. He learned what not to say (usually after it was too late and his foot was firmly inserted into his mouth) and to always put the toilet seat down. He learned the difference between the playful and light "Chad," the are-you-kidding "Chaaaad," and the serious "Chadwick." I taught him how to eat leftovers, and we built up a tolerance for a thousand recipes with Spam. Spam and beans with maple syrup was his favorite.

Chad introduced me to sleeping with the window open – even in the dead of winter – and the pure, exhilarating pleasure of waking up with snow on your nose, going to Dairy Queen during a blizzard, sleeping in the nude (although I never bought into that one), and shopping and doing laundry at three in the morning.

We learned about budgeting, meal planning, bill paying, stretching paychecks, entertaining ourselves, sale searching, coupon clipping, taking naps, afternoon delight, and just plain old relaxing.

We managed to do a lot together despite our crazy schedules, always starting with a cup of coffee in the morning when we could, and ending with us tucking each other in at night. We were happy and comfortable in that little three-room apartment.

Our first Christmas season brought us our greatest gift. I remember the night we became pregnant. After making love, Chad stroked my hair as he loved to do and whispered excitedly, "Tonight we created a new life."

I could only respond, "I know."

That could have been wishful thinking, but a couple of days later, my mood was down. Chad asked me what was wrong, and I blurted out that I "knew" I was pregnant, but "you spoiled the good news. I wanted to be the one to tell you that the rabbit died."

Everything was confirmed, and it was time to face the realities of parenthood. I mean, I was barely twenty-one, and Chad had just turned twenty-two. What did we know about being parents?

Well, like those before us and those who came after us, it was a learning experience on the fly. I worried about things like not having a crib. Chad worried about having another mouth to feed. But we got through it. I graduated with a little baby bump. On September 8, 1969, at 4:12 p.m., Chadwick William Watt, Jr. joined the world. We opted to call him JR.

We could take JR anywhere and he would sleep. Other than during potty training, he was a perfect introduction to parenthood. Still, his arrival forced us to look for a larger two-bedroom apartment on base. Moving into the apartment marked the end of our honeymoon. When we moved out, we were starting a new beginning in our lives.

I worked for a little while before JR was born, but Chad said my job was to take care of our son. I took this job seriously.

We took a vacation in 1971 to Lake George in the Adirondacks of New York. Hectic days at Frontier Town and petting zoos were capped with nights under the stars overlooking the lake. We stayed in a one-room cabin, and I was busy rearranging the furniture shortly after we arrived. I moved a couple of chairs onto the porch, and that was our nightly sanctuary. I would make a pot of coffee, and we would unwind while JR slept inside. We would just sit for hours, talking about the first couple of years of our marriage and our future. We had never had a vacation that relaxing of before.

I was in an upbeat mood. I thought it was the clean air, but as we were getting ready to go back home, I walked to the car with JR in my arms and gave Chad a big hug and kiss. Out of nowhere, I added, "I'm not sure, but I think I'm pregnant."

I was, and it was a rough pregnancy. Chad had to go to Colorado for a few weeks. He called every night, but I never told him how I really felt. I spotted for a couple of days, but I didn't tell anyone. I didn't even call my doctor.

That changed as soon as Chad walked through the door. He immediately called my doctor and whisked me off to the emergency room. Everything seemed okay, but the doctor ordered bed rest for a couple of weeks – something nearly impossible with a two-year-old running around.

Still, we got through it, and we cried tears of joy when Katelyn Danielle Watt was introduced to the world on January 25, 1972, at 4:12 a.m.

We had birthday parties and watched JR and Kate-D grow. We played cards with our neighbors, always welcoming a steady stream of friends into the apartment.

Kate-D was impossible; she didn't want to sleep anywhere except in her crib, so we never went out. She was also a rocker, and she put her head through the crib headboard. Meanwhile, JR was a typical toddler, getting into everything, including repainting the living room walls with butter. The two urchins wore me down.

Chad noticed a new housing development going up. He packed us up, and we went to see the area. The land was just being cleared; there was only one "show home" and a couple of others under construction. We went through the figures and calculations. Since the house was under construction, we could "save" some money by not adding a gambrel roof and doing our own painting. All we needed was $7,000 down.

Chad and I went through every possible scenario to get our payments in line. If we sold the car ... if we scrimped here and there ... if we. ... I'll admit I was less enthusiastic and more realistic. If we sold the car, we would have to get another one. Even if we scrimped and saved, the pennies wouldn't add up fast enough.

Somehow, the pieces fell into place. Chad was promoted in rank and pay. We found a buyer for the Chevy wagon and a reliable replacement, which meant no more car payments. We kept filling our water jug with loose change, and we culled as many extras from the house as we could, like a finished basement, painting, landscaping other than basic seeding, and the gambrel roof over the door. The mortgage application somehow went through. We were going to be new homeowners!

We closed in late 1974. After a check for the escrow ... and another for the taxes ... and another for the insurance ... and another for the points ... and another for I don't remember what, we were both in shock. When we got back to the car, all I could ask was, "What did we just get ourselves into? Are we going to be okay?"

Chad said, "Sure we are." It all turned out fine – just don't ask me how.

We managed to get some of the work done around the house. Chad was a good engineer, but he was not as handy with a hammer or screwdriver. Still, he framed a patio and had it poured, although it had a slight pitch. (Okay, a marble would roll right off it.) He also finished a room in the basement. (Okay, it had a gaping hole in the closet, and he never did find his hammer after putting up the wallboard.) I always teased him about being able to design detailed plans but not being able to follow them. I sure was glad he was designing and not building projects for the Air Force!

We finally got the fireplace we had to scrub when the house was built, and my forsythia twigs matured into a vibrant break on the edge of our property line. We even got a puppy, a playful Irish Setter named Harrigan, who fit right in with the family.

Chad spent a lot of time with the kids. He taught JR how to fish, usually with Kate-D tugging at his pant leg, pleading, "Can I go too, Daddy? Please!"

One day I came home from shopping and found Chad sitting on the floor "drinking" tea with his four-year-old daughter. There was Little League and Brownies and boys' weekends and dance recitals.

Like he had when we were dating, he listened patiently to my words and my heart. He gave me his prime time, not the leftovers. He praised me. He surprised me. He continued to court me. He treated me like a queen in front of other people.

Even though we were a military family, life still seemed normal. Since Chad worked on projects with mostly civilian engineers, there weren't many Air Force rules to deal with. He had most weekends and holidays off.

But one time in 1977, he and his team had to go to Schriever Air Force Base in Colorado Springs to integrate their portion of a satellite-monitoring project with other teams from around the country. What was supposed to be a six-week assignment dragged to over six months. We missed being together at Thanksgiving, and it looked like we were going to miss Christmas as well.

Somehow, Chad found a friend of a friend of a friend who couldn't use their condo in Aspen over the Christmas holiday. He called and asked me if I wanted to celebrate Christmas in Colorado. I had about a million reasons why we shouldn't, but I sure did miss him, and I knew the kids did too. We thought about flying, but I decided to drive the three days and 1,200 miles with a five-year-old and an eight-year-old. It was quite an adventure, navigating unpredictable weather and trying to keep JR and Kate-D occupied, but it was worth it.

Chad brought a Christmas tree and decorated it, which greeted us when we arrived. We spent our days skiing, sledding, and building snowmen. We drank gallons of hot chocolate. We not only celebrated Christmas, but JR's and Kate-D's birthdays as well. At night after the kids were settled in, Chad and I snuggled in front of the fireplace (and then some). It was like a second honeymoon.

Of course, all good things come to an end, and the kids and I returned home. Chad finally made it back on Valentine's Day, holding a dozen red roses. He never ceased to amaze me.

Later in the summer, Chad and I were in the PX military store doing some shopping. Out of the blue, he said, "Do you think we should start going to church?"

Stunned, I stopped in my tracks. "What?"

"Do you think we should start going to church?" he repeated.

"Is something wrong? Are you okay?" I answered instinctively, thinking he might be melancholic since we had just buried his father a couple of months before after a sudden heart attack.

"I'm fine," he insisted. "Forget it. I just thought the kids should start learning about God."

Now, Chad and I had been brought up in the church, and we were believers. But we never really practiced our faith after we got married beyond attending Christmas or Easter services and weddings and funerals.

"I'm not against it," I said as I pushed our wobbly-wheeled cart back down the aisle. "You just caught me off guard. Why don't we get a coffee and talk about it?"

That's exactly what we did. Chad explained that faith and church attendance had become a fairly regular topic in the office. He thought it might be time to do something. After all, he reasoned, JR was almost ten and Kate-D was almost seven. "We know what we believe, but what about them?"

"Sure, hon. We can go to church. That was never an issue. I just wanted to make sure you're okay, that's all," I said.

Since we had both grown up in the Catholic church, I figured we would be heading to St. Paul's down the street, but Chad suggested Grace Community Church in Huber Heights, about twelve miles away. He said a couple of the members of his team went there and they spoke about it favorably.

I was skeptical, but we packed up the kids and went to the 10:50 contemporary service on Sunday morning. The kids went off to children's church, and Chad and I encountered a totally different worship experience. Everyone was friendly and helpful. The church had a casual atmosphere with a message that focused on our relationship with Jesus, not a bunch of rules and regulations. It had uplifting music rather than stale hymns, and horns and drums replaced the organ. I couldn't speak for Chad, but I left with a warm feeling.

Chad suggested we stop at IHOP after the service, and we went around the table, sharing our views about the church. The kids were just as enthusiastic as I was, and over our pancakes, we decided to make this a Sunday tradition.

Over the next few months, we got more involved at Grace with Bible studies and family-focused activities, and the kids got involved in AWANA. Chad and I found new friends and a home outside of our home.

Of course, not everyone approved of our decision. Chad's mom and my dad tolerated the decision, but Mom was ... well ... Mom. How could I do such a thing? How could I turn away from God? What was she supposed to tell Father Pat or her friends?

We headed home to visit our parents for Easter 1979. When we arrived, Chad complained about a headache. I gave him aspirin and all seemed well. By midweek, however, he was again complaining of a headache. Again, the aspirin did its magic.

Still, headaches were unusual for Captain Watt. He was in good shape, and he regularly passed his physicals with flying colors. Chad having multiple bouts with headaches in a week was a source of concern for me, although they weren't constant, and they were easily managed with aspirin.

When he continued to complain over the next few weeks, however, I suggested that he get his eyes checked. He agreed, and sure enough, he was now a candidate for glasses. When he went to get the specs fitted, however, the doctor brushed the side of his head just above the ear. Chad said the casual contact resulted in an immediate deep migraine. The eye doctor discovered swelling just under the hairline and told Chad – and me when I came to pick him up – that it should be checked.

42

So we headed to the doctor. The news was not good. After multiple tests, Chad was diagnosed with a glioblastoma multiforme tumor, one of the fastest-growing cancers of the brain, and the deadliest. It had already started to grow, and Chad started feeling worse and worse. Ultimately, he had a seizure that sent him to the hospital over Memorial Day weekend. Dr. Walker scheduled a surgery to take out a section of the tumor for a pathological diagnosis and to remove some of the mass pressing against his brain. He said we would follow with radiotherapy and chemotherapy. But the prognosis, he warned, was not good. Chad's age and physical shape were a plus, but the typical survival expectancy was only about a year.

Our parents flew in. JR and Kate-D were lost, and there wasn't much I could do to help them. I was lost too, stunned and shocked by the sudden turn of events.

We had a chance to talk and pray before Chad went into surgery. We walked down memory lane, and he told me that he never regretted a moment of our time together.

"I knew," he said, "you were my soul mate the first time I talked to you in that club in New York. I told you that you were the most beautiful girl I had seen."

I reminded him that he had also added "tonight."

"I may have said that, but I meant *ever*. You had such a special, quirky honesty about you. I fell in love you right then, right there."

"You say the sweetest things. You always know how to make a girl feel special."

"I tried."

"No. *Try*. Don't give up. Don't ever give up, not on yourself, not on me, not on the kids."

"I promise."

He also said he was sorry.

"For what?" I asked.

"For this. For making you go through this. For everything I ever did to hurt you. I never meant to," he said.

I hushed him and held him as tight as I could amid the wires and tubing. "You ... never ... hurt ... me. You ... always ... loved ... me ... unconditionally," I sobbed. "Get ... through ... the ... surgery ... tomorrow. One ... day ... at ... a ... time."

Dr. Walker was less optimistic after the surgery. He said the fingerlike tentacles of the tumor couldn't be removed, and that they were growing into the temporal lobe, cerebellum, and dangerously close to the brain stem. "I'm sorry," he said. "I think we should consider palliative care."

Chad wasn't Chad after the surgery. He had a hard time focusing or recognizing people and places. But he always held my hand, squeezing it between pangs of pain. He died on June 12, 1979 at 12:35 p.m., a day after our eleventh anniversary, with me holding him tight and telling him, "I love you." Dr. Walker had given us six months. I had gotten sixteen days.

I don't remember much about the calling hours or funeral. I remember keeping my children close under my wing as we greeted an endless line of visitors, but I couldn't tell you who they were or what they said. I was surprised by the number of people who showed up to pay their respects to Captain Watt, both military and civilian. He had touched so many lives.

There he was, decked in his dress uniform, surreally sleeping in his high-gloss red cherry casket on almond velvet sheets. An honor guard stood at the corners, watching over my fallen hero.

Pastor Rick officiated the service and eulogized Chad. I can't remember all of what he said, but I do remember him saying that a person's life is like the residue left after drinking a glass of milk. You have to scrub it to remove its effect, he said. Otherwise, it stays on the glass. A quick rinse can't remove it. I don't remember where he was going with the analogy, but it did resonate with me. Chad's "milk" had left its mark on the world.

At the cemetery, all I could do was stare at that flag-draped casket. I don't know whether I was squeezing JR's and Kate-D's hands or if they were squeezing mine. The three of us accepted his folded flag, and even though I had been to many military funerals, the staccato of rifle volleys stunned me to my core. Maybe it was the sudden sound amid the eerie silence. My parents and Chad's mom took the kids while I sat there for what felt like forever, not wanting to leave. The casket took on strange shapes and hues through the lens of my teary eyes. Dad came back from the car to get me, and I completely broke down in his arms.

I was still in a fog at home, politely greeting friends but wanting to be anywhere but there. My parents and Chad's mother stayed for about a week, and we decided to let the kids go back with them. We figured the grandparents could keep them occupied while I went through the mundane chores of new widowhood. I'm still not sure if that was the right decision, for the kids or myself.

I didn't sleep well. Okay, I hardly slept at all. I didn't eat right. It was too much trouble cooking for one, or to even go to the well-stocked freezer for something quick and easy. I broke down in the silence of the house. I couldn't watch the television shows Chad and I had watched together. My first trip to the PX ended three steps inside the door. I just couldn't go on.

There were many forms to be filled out, and even the simplest forms took me hours to complete. I had to focus to make sure the check for the electric company actually went into the envelope for the electric company. I cried every time I wrote a check that still had Chad's name atop mine, and I cried every time I went to the mailbox and found mail addressed to both of us. I cried whenever anything triggered a memory, and almost everything did.

CHAPTER FIVE

I PICKED UP the kids in mid-August. When I got to Mom and Dad's house, Mom greeted me with, "Samantha, you look like shit!"

Thanks, Mom. I feel like shit, but I was hoping for a better greeting than that.

JR and Kate-D ran up and gave me big hugs. That was better. When Dad got home from work, he cradled me in his arms like he used to do when I was a little girl. "Love you, pumpkin," he whispered, causing my eyes to flood, and his too.

When I went to Mom Watt's home, she greeted me warmly and lectured me over a cup of tea about taking care of myself. I love my mother-in-law, but all I heard was, "Blah blah blah, blah blah de blah."

I went to lunch with Bernie and Lynn, and the two of them tried desperately to get me to go down to the shore over the weekend, "just like we used to do." I declined.

"There's too many memories," I told them. I don't think they understood, but they respected my decision, although Bernie stopped by Mom and Dad's a couple of times. She had been a good, close, let's-talk-over-coffee type friend for so many years.

I only stayed for a couple of days before we headed home. The kids had to get ready for school. It was a quiet ride home, with none of us talking or playing license plate bingo or "I spy" like we generally did on car rides.

I don't know why I rushed home. It wasn't a home anymore, just bricks and mortar, wood and nails, a house. Even the normal commotion of two young kids couldn't penetrate the eerie silence within the walls.

I still wasn't sleeping well, and I knew we weren't eating right. It wasn't unusual for either JR or Kate-D to find me crying. I still couldn't watch television at night, and I wasn't focused enough to even read. So I paced, puttered around the house, or sat in the darkened living room doing nothing, which would get me to thinking about Chad and all we had done and all we had planned to do, which drove me deeper into my despair.

That all changed on September 12, three months to the day after Chad died. The night before was like so many others. For whatever reason, instead of wearing my pajamas, I had on one of Chad's old shirts; I just couldn't get rid of them. I couldn't sleep. After tossing and turning for hours, I made my way to the couch and curled up in the fetal position, covered by the Cincinnati Bengals blanket that was usually on the back of Chad's recliner.

I must have dozed off, and in that suspended state, I heard JR telling Kate-D to be quiet. Without opening my eyes, I heard him pour cereal for his sister in the kitchen. She asked who was going to brush her hair. He told her he would do it, and I heard a muffled, "Ow," followed by a whispered, "I'm sorry!" as he discovered a knot. Kate-D said just as quietly, "That's okay." They came over by me and blew me kisses as they headed for the door, but I was incapable of responding. I tried, but my eyes and mouth and body remained motionless.

I was in that same fetal position when they came home. I didn't hear them come in, but I felt JR gently stroking my arm. "Mom? Mom? Are you okay?" he said quietly with a tinge of fear in his voice.

As I finally opened my eyes, I saw Kate-D standing next to him with tears streaming from her eyes. "Mom?" he asked again as I managed to pull my arm from under the blanket. "Are you okay?"

"Yes, sweetie, I'm okay," I said.

"You scared us, Mommy," he said, with Kate-D parroting him, "You scared us, Mommy. We thought we lost you too."

That woke me up. I gathered them up like a mother hen with her chicks under her wing. "I'm okay. I'm sorry. I didn't mean to scare you," I assured them.

With JR hugging me from my left and Kate-D from my right, I embraced both of them in a group hug. All I could say was, "I love you. I love you," as I kissed each of them on their head. I could have lived in that moment forever.

"Give me a couple of minutes to get dressed," I told them, "then we'll go out for dinner. Where do you want to go?"

Without hesitation and with gigantic smiles on their faces, they said "IHOP!"

Kate-D added, "Can I have pancakes?"

When I said, "Sure," Kate-D responded, "Yeah! Just like when we go with Da–"

She stopped mid-word, realizing what she was about to say. JR turned with a stern, "Kate!"

"It's okay," I said. "Yeah, just like when we went with Daddy. Give me a couple minutes to get dressed and we'll go to IHOP, just like the old days."

That's what we did. Breakfast for dinner. Over the pancakes and sausage, I realized how I had failed to let the kids talk about how they were feeling about Chad's death. I was so wrapped up in myself that I'd forgotten about them and their hurt and grief. We talked about the happy times with Chad. "Remember when ..." became a common preface as they each shared stories.

When we got home, we gathered around the table and talked some more. When it became too melancholic, I packed them up and we walked down the street for some ice cream. We got home, and I told them to get into their pj's and brush their teeth. I had another surprise for them.

As they were getting ready for bed, I got into my pajamas as well. When they came to kiss me goodnight, I told them we were sleeping together in my bed.

"We can talk about Daddy, about how you're feeling, about school, about anything you want," I told them. "Tonight is for you. Okay?"

They loved the idea. They snuggled with me. We shared our feelings. There were plenty of tears, but there was plenty of laughter. I got a front-row seat into what they were going through and how I had con-tributed to their angst. It wasn't always pretty. For the first time in three months, they had an opportunity to share their thoughts and feelings.

We talked for hours. Kate-D gave in first, falling asleep around eleven. JR hung on for another hour or so. Despite having knees in my back and an arm slung over my face, it was the best night's sleep I had in months.

The next day after I dropped the kids off at school, I stopped in at the guidance office at Wright State. I figured if I needed to move on, I should probably take a refresher nursing course and get my certification. While waiting for the guidance counselor, I picked up the local weekly newspaper sitting on one of the tables. By happenstance – although, is there ever truly happenstance? – there was an ad announcing a grief counseling series at Miami Valley Hospital, the same hospital where Chad had died. I wasn't sure I could step back in there, but I also knew I couldn't go on this way. So, I jotted down the number and signed up.

I had opportunities for grief counseling through the Air Force, but I knew so many military families. I didn't want to expose myself to people I knew. When I walked into the chapel for the meeting, I still wasn't sure it was the right route to go. Yet, when I looked around and saw the grief on my fellow travelers' faces and heard our grief counselor, Gail's, reassuring voice, I knew I was among friends.

It was painful. I was the rookie of the group – the youngest and the most recently widowed. I allowed the others to step up as I qui-etly listened. One woman had nursed her husband for years while he was battling cancer. Another had lost her husband to a heart attack. A woman and her daughter had lost a son and brother to suicide. A man had come home from work and found his wife dead at the bottom of the stairs. When it was my turn, I offered my tale of woe, and like the others before me, I shared my story through plenty of tears. As I drove home, it dawned on me: I was blessed. I'd had a chance to say good-bye, and I knew that Chad hadn't suffered long.

Gail kept us on track and touched raw nerves while helping us understand the chaotic emotions we were going through. She played the song "Be Still" by the Celebrant Singers that first night and replayed it at our last session when the slight variation in the lyrics made sense. Over the years, whenever I feel myself spinning out of control, I remember those words from Psalm 46:10, *Be still and know that I am God.*

CHAPTER SIX

C-R-A-S-H!

"Shit!"

The crash and shrill comment awakened me from my nostalgic Neverland and brought back into reality.

"Mom?" I cried out, at the same time realizing my hands were immersed mid-forearm in soapy water.

"I'm okay," Mom said. "I just knocked over a table."

Simultaneously, I cried out again, "Mom, are you all right?"

"Yes, I'm fine," she repeated as I fumbled for a dish towel and headed into the living room.

There she was, on all fours on the floor, picking up a thousand jigsaw pieces. I noticed a wet spot on her behind, shadowed by a slightly larger dried stain. I righted the table and helped her scoop the pieces back into the box. Then, trying to be discreet and sympathetic as I helped her back to her feet, I said, "Mom, you must have spilled something. Let's –"

"Or I pissed myself again," she interrupted.

"Well, let's get you cleaned up. Then I'll make some tea, okay?"

"Okay," she said. She squeezed my hand, and we made our way into the bedroom.

The bedroom. Now, Mom was never Mrs. Homemaker. Her forte was working in the kitchen. Yet, when I walked into her room, I was aghast. The bed wasn't made, there were clothes thrown on it and the floor, drawers were half opened with clothes hanging out, and shoes and slippers littered the floor. It looked more like ... well ... my room when I was a teenager.

As she started changing, I went into the bathroom. The hamper was overflowing, powder was all over the floor, the shower curtain liner was all bunched up with flecks of mold in the creases, and the medicine chest was wide open.

When I got back to the kitchen to put water on for tea, I was overwhelmed by not only the dishes, glasses, and cups I had washed and dried, but also with how many more still had to be done. Where had they come from?

It had been just a few weeks since I'd been home visiting, then burying Dad. I guess I had been so wrapped up with him that I'd neglected to take notice of Mom. And in that moment, I remembered my last conversation with Dad.

"You have to promise me something, sweetheart," he said.

"Anything, Daddy," I responded through tears. "You know that."

"You have to take care of Mom."

"Of course."

"No, I mean it," he said sternly in a tone I rarely heard from him. "I know you and Mom don't always get along, but she's a good woman."

"Well, I know," I said.

"Believe it or not, you two are so much alike. But she is going to need you. Give her a chance, and promise me you will take care of her."

As Mom appeared in the kitchen and sat down at the dining room table, I hardly recognized her. How had she aged so much in just a few weeks? What was going on?

The nurse in me led me to tackle the parade of orange bottles sitting over the sink. Most of them were probably Dad's. I figured I would weed his out and take them down to the pharmacy for disposal.

Sure enough, the first five or so were Dad's. But there were still a number of bottles left, along with aspirin and vitamins. They were for Mom. *Okay, potassium. That makes sense. After all, Mom is seventy-six years old. Metformin. That must be for her diabetes. All right, furosemide, a diuretic. Whoa, Norvasc. I know Mom has high blood pressure, but that's a pretty potent dose. Huh? More high blood pressure meds? Lisinopril? What in the world is this? Aricept. Isn't that for dementia? When was Mom diagnosed with dementia?*

"Mom. Mom," I called out.

"Yes, dear?"

"Have you been taking your meds?"

"Yes," she said confidently. I looked at the bottles again. When I checked fill dates, the number of pills that had been used didn't match it.

"Are you sure?" I asked as I carried the bottles into the living room. "I haven't seen you take any pills since I've been here."

"You just didn't see me," she responded, flicking her hand dismissively.

I sat down next to her. "Mom. What's going on? What are these all for?"

"I don't know," she said candidly. "The doctor said I needed to take them, so I do."

"But do you know why? Do you know what you're being treated for? What's the Aricept for? Are you being treated for dementia?"

"No. No," she said. "I forget things sometimes. These are just to help me remember."

"Well, how are you feeling?" I continued.

"I'm tired ... real tired."

She also looked a little pale, so I pulled out my stethoscope to take her blood pressure. Even though she balked at first, she let me take it. Eighty-eight over fifty-two, which was too low – much too low. No wonder she looked pale and was so tired.

"Okay, on Monday I'm calling Dr. Gibson. I need to know how you're doing and what you're being treated for," I told her.

Sheepishly, she responded, "Whatever."

It was the morning of Mother's Day. In the early hours, I read my daily devotional, which focused on Titus 2:3–5, a passage telling older women to teach what is good so that they may encourage the young women to love their husbands, to love their children, to be self-controlled, chaste, good managers of the household, kind, being submissive to their husbands, so that the Word of God may not be discredited.

The devotional read, "The scope of what the younger women need to learn cannot be communicated in words. It is action. It is an older woman who bakes beautifully, whose garden is spectacular. It is the kind of thing that faithful living communicates. It encourages younger women more than you can know. It gives hope toward the future. It gives ideas and inspiration for what kind of women we want to be. But it gives it in a way that is discreet, that encourages without pressuring. It gives it in a way that is not an invitation to complain about your life or fuss about your children. It is encouragement in the best way, encouragement by example."

As I was reading, I heard Mom call out, "Samantha! Samantha!" I immediately stopped and went across the hall to her room.

"What's wrong, Mom?"

"I just wanted to know you were still here. I don't want to be alone. Can you sit with me?"

"Of course," I said, reaching over to give her a kiss on the cheek. "Happy Mother's Day."

"Oh, Happy Mother's Day to you, dear."

"Do you want some tea? Do you want me to make you some breakfast?"

"No, I just want you to sit with me."

"Okay," I responded, "but I am going to take your vitals. You look awfully pale."

Her blood pressure was still low, and I could feel her body temperature was lower than normal. I'd seen the signs before. This wasn't going to be a long journey.

We sat there, me holding her hand for minutes, although it felt like hours. She drifted in and out of sleep.

Suddenly, out of the blue, she patted my hand and said, "Sam, I'm sorry if I ever hurt you. I love you. I have always loved you."

"Shhh," I said. "I know you've always loved me, and I've always loved you."

"But we never told each other, did we?" she said. "I'm sorry for that."

"I am too," I answered.

"Why not?" she asked. "Why weren't we close? Why didn't we ever talk about it before?"

I crinkled my nose and simply responded, "I don't know."

Mom, despite her increasingly shallow breaths, said she wanted to make me strong and independent. "You had your dad wrapped around your little finger, and I had to be the mean mom. I had to be the one to say no."

"You weren't mean," I interjected. "But you could be hurtful, almost like my feelings didn't matter. That's what bothered me the most. I mean, I could get straight A's and you would focus on my lone B. I didn't think I was ever good enough for you," I added, my eyes welling up. "But I always loved and respected you."

"I'm sorry, sweetheart," she said. "I tried to make you strong and inde-pendent." She tried to smile, adding, "I think I was successful. Maybe too successful. You're the strongest, most independent woman I know. And that scared me."

"I'm not that strong," I said. "I'm not independent."

"Well, I'm proud of you. You're a survivor. That's all a mom can ask for."

She drifted off again, so I got dressed, made some tea, and warmed up a couple of muffins. I also called Dr. Gibson just to let him know what was going on. When he called back, all he could say was, "Keep her comfortable."

As I walked back into her room, she half-opened her eyes. She wanted no part of the muffin, but she did drink some tea through a straw.

"I'm so tired," she said. "But I want you to just sit with me and talk to me. We missed that over the years."

"Of course. What do you want to talk about? Anything special?"

"How did you get through everything?"

"What do you mean?"

"Putting up with me while growing up. Burying ..." she said, trying to remember, "your husband ... uh. ..."

"Chad."

"Yes, Chad. I should have been there for you."

"Mom, there was nothing you or anyone could do. I had to work through it myself. Taking care of the kids was a big help."

"How are the kids doing? JR looks just like his dad, and Kate looks just like you."

"They're doing okay. You just saw them a couple of weeks ago at Dad's funeral."

"I know, but I didn't spend much time with them."

"Well, JR always dreamed of following in his dad's footsteps. He joined the Air Force ROTC program at Bowling Green, and he is now a commissioned officer. Unlike his father, though, he is a pilot," I reported. "The deployments cost him his first marriage, but he and Heather had two girls, Rachel and Nancy. He's doing more teaching than flying now, and he has gotten remarried, to Bekah. They have a son, Chad III, and a daughter, Diana.

"Kate followed my nursing footsteps, although she was harder to get out of my nest. She went to Wright State, but she stayed at home until she got married to a fine young man, Al, at age twenty-six and moved to Toledo. She has two children, a boy, John, and a girl, Kathi."

Mom interrupted me. "Did Kate give you trouble like you gave me?"

I laughed. "No. She wasn't as flirty as I was. But I was always a good girl. I may have pushed the envelope, but I set boundaries I wouldn't cross. That's because of you, Mom."

I told her that Kate was the "fixer." "She spent a lot of time trying to take care of me. She would try to set me up on dates with her friends' fathers or uncles."

"What about you?" Mom asked. "Why didn't you ever get remarried? Knowing how outgoing you were growing up, I thought for sure you would find someone else."

"I was never interested," I said. "Chad and I had something special. I knew it could never be replicated. I mean, I went out on a couple of dates, but it just wasn't the same."

"What about your neighbor?" she asked.

"George? He's been a special friend. He lost his wife a couple months before Chad died. JR and his son, Georgie, were best friends, so George made sure he included JR in camping, Scouting, and other guy activities. He helped me around the house, and we often would accompany each other to events. Not as dates, though. We've been special friends ... wow ... for thirty-four years."

"What about Ber ... Bet ... Betsy?" Mom asked.

"You mean Bernie?"

"Yeah," she said. "I was never sure whether she was a bad influence on you or you were a bad influence on her."

I laughed. "Bernie and I have been tight forever! She's doing okay. She still lives here in Jersey, and she operates a hair salon. We talk all the time. In fact, we'll probably get together before I head back."

"Thank you," Mom said. "This was nice. Just talking with you. Just having you here with me."

"Yes, it was nice. Why don't you rest a little? And remember, I love you."

"Okay," Mom said. "I love you too, and I'm so proud of the woman you've become."

That was our last conversation. Shortly after noon, I felt Mom's hand go limp in mine, and I knew it was over. I lifted her up and held her in my arms. She had a smile on her face, which put a smile on my crying face. She was home, and we both were at peace.

CHAPTER SEVEN

EVEN THOUGH HE was retired, Father Pat concelebrated Mom's Mass of Christian Burial and offered the homily. An octogenarian himself, he had known Mom for over fifty years, first as a young priest in the parish, and later returning as pastor.

During the homily, he looked straight at me. "Samantha, your mom was so proud of you. Every Sunday she would tell me, 'Sam did this,' or 'Sam did that.' I watched you grow up, not only myself, but through the eyes of your mother. Even when you made questionable choices, it was your mother who defended you. She was behind you all the way from grade school through high school and into college. She always told me what you were doing in Ohio and about your family. She may not have said it, but she loved you so very much."

Normally, being singled out like that would have made me squirm. I may have even challenged some of those comments. But I had sat with Mom over those last hours, and I knew Father Pat was spot-on. A smile appeared on my face, and I looked over at the casket. I could almost see Mom smiling as well.

I found myself driving home alone on the black asphalt, which seemed darker because of ominous clouds again on the horizon ranging from dark gray to puffs of white. Out of the corner of my eye, I caught a glimpse of white as the sun tried to peek out from behind the clouds. It didn't succeed, but first a ray rained into the picture, followed by a halo of rays.

I remembered my conversations with the kids when we had seen a similar canvas in the sky that day. They'd thought the light was heaven shining through.

I knew they were right.

The End.

CPSIA information can be obtained
at www.ICGtesting.com
Printed in the USA
FFOW04n1225100418
46222871-47552FF